Beach Reads
Boozy Book Club Series
by
Rose Bak

# Also by Rose Bak

**Bite-Sized Shifters**
Long Distance Wolf
Wolf Doctor
Kat's Dog
Designer Wolf
Wolf Sheriff
Cocktail Wolf
Second Chance Wolf

**Boozy Book Club**
Beach Reads
Bubbly & Billionaires: A Midlife Instalove Romantic Comedy
Martinis & Mysteries

**Diamond Bay**
Brand New Penny
Fresh as a Daisy
Right as Rain

**Good With Numbers**
Love Unmasked
The Thanksgiving Scrooge
Maid for Christmas
Countdown to Love
Valentine's Lottery

**Holidays With the Shifters**
Santa's Claws
Bear Humbug
Jingle Bear
Joy to the Wolf
Lion's Heart
Silver Paws

**Loving the Holidays**
Dating Santa
New Year's Steve
Independence Dave

**Magical Midlife Romance**
Love Potion

**Oliver Boys Band**

Until You Came Along
Rock Star Teacher
Rock Star Writer
Rock Star Neighbor


**Reunited**
Together Again
Finding My Baby


**Self-Help for the Real World**
It's All About Relationships


**Standalone**
What to Do If You Find a Cougar in Your Living Room
Beach Wedding
Good with Numbers
Christmas Love Stories: A Holiday Romance Anthology
Diamond Bay
Christmas with the Shifters


Watch for more at https://rosebakenterprises.com/.

# Table of Contents

---

1.      https://paperorpixels.com/

# About this book

**She was supposed to be celebrating her sister's birthday, not falling in love with some guy she just met!**

When her sister invites her on a girls' weekend to celebrate her fiftieth birthday, Teresa tries her best to get out of it. She's much too busy to take a vacation, let alone spend time with the charming and sexy bartender at the resort they're visiting.

Colin never believed in love at first sight, at least until he set eyes on Teresa. The curvy beauty is everything he's ever wanted in a woman. If he could just convince her to stay...but first, he needs to tell her the truth about who he really is.

"Beach Reads" is a prequel novella in the "Boozy Book Club" series. Each story in the series is a steamy standalone featuring a couple over forty-five, a nosy group of matchmaking friends, and a sweet happily ever after that proves anyone can find love later in life.

*This book includes a special excerpt from "Until You Came Along", book one of the Oliver Boys Rockstar series, available now from all major online retailers.*

# Author's Note

*An earlier version of this story appeared in "Beat the Heat", a limited edition anthology.*

# Join My Mailing List

**Click here[1] to join Rose Bak's mailing list. You'll get a free book and be the first to hear about all the latest releases and special sales.**

# Dedication

*For everyone who works a little too hard, loves a little too much, and isn't afraid to chuck it all.*

# Prologue—Teresa

"Mom, I told you, I don't have time for this."

"I don't care. It's only four days. Three and a half really. You can make time for your sister on her special day." Her voice softened. "It's important to her to have you there."

"I don't know why." Even I could hear the poutiness in my voice, as if I were thirteen instead of forty-three. "She'll have Emma and Dawn there. She doesn't need me."

My older sister Evie was turning fifty and she had decided to have a girls' weekend at a resort in the Florida Keys. Why I had to be one of the girls, I wasn't sure. Don't get me wrong, I appreciated the offer, but my sister and I were not particularly close. In fact, we were as different as night and day.

Seven years older than me, Evie was embracing the outrageousness of middle age. She was a serial dater and a chronic flirt who was also loud, unspoken, and prone to dying her hair weird colors. Lately we had seen that she also had some business savvy. After years of bouncing from job to job, she had recently bought a bookstore, turning it into a popular community gathering place and a thriving business. In this day of e-books, that was no small feat.

My sister was always throwing herself into what she called "adventures". For Evie, everything was an adventure. She could have an adventure going grocery shopping. And turning fifty was going to be her biggest adventure.

"Come on, Teri Bear," she'd wheedled, pulling out the childish nickname she had saddled me with as a baby. "We're going to go ziplining and parasailing and snorkeling and dancing."

"Even if I could take time off from work, which I can't right now, there's no way I would do all that crazy stuff."

I was the cautious one in the family. Evie liked to joke that I didn't even go to the bathroom without conducting an analysis and putting it on my schedule. The truth was, I was one of those Type A people. I was always working, always planning, always meticulous in everything I did.

"You don't have to do anything you don't want to, but I know that you haven't had a vacation in years. You need a break. Just imagine how great it would be spending the entire day on the beach, reading and drinking frozen cocktails."

My sister was not wrong about me needing a break, and I couldn't deny that relaxing on a sunny beach sounded like heaven. I hadn't taken a vacation in so long I was maxed out on vacation time at work. Our human resources director had sent me an email recently advising me that I was no longer accruing any new time off and needed to "evaluate ways to have more appropriate work/life balance" – code for "take a damn vacation."

"Teresa Ann Fontenot," my mother interrupted my train of thought. "You will not disappoint your sister. She asks so little from you."

I sighed. It was true. Evie was a great sister, always there for me when I needed her. I supposed four days away would be doable, especially when two of those days were the weekend. If I caught an early flight back on Monday I would really only miss work on Friday. Plus, I could bring my laptop and work from one of those beach cabanas. In fact, the more I thought about it, the more I realized that a change of scenery would be nice, especially right now when it was cold and dreary here in New York City.

"Fine, I'll go," I said grudgingly.

"Good girl."

I rolled my eyes. I only hoped I was not going to regret this.

# Colin

I wiped down the bar and ignored the suggestive looks the blonde in the tiny bikini was shooting my way. After all these years working at the Hamilton Keys Resort, I knew the look of a woman on the prowl. I noted the tan lines on her ring finger and idly wondered if she was recently divorced or having a weekend away from her husband. Either way I wasn't interested. She was much too young for me, and much too artificial. From her tits to her lips to her hair extensions, there didn't seem to be any original parts on this one. Not to mention the fact that the entire top of her face was unnaturally still, as if she'd had one too many Botox injections.

I heard voices and turned to see a group of women gathering at one of the tables. The beachfront bar was a favorite for the guests who stayed at the resort. Mere yards from the ocean, it was a good place to watch the waves and rehydrate while staying out of the sun.

I threw a bar towel over my shoulder and ambled over to the table, checking out the newcomers. Three ladies who looked like they were in their forties, and one younger one, maybe thirty-five or so. I wasn't super good at estimating women's ages, but all four had some years on them, which I appreciated. At forty-eight, I liked a woman with some mileage. At this age, they knew their own mind and weren't so baby obsessed like the younger women were.

"What can I get—-."

My words sputtered out as my eyes locked with the younger woman at the table. She was stunning. She had dark brown hair that fell just above her shoulders in what I knew was an expensive bob. Chocolate brown eyes squinted at me as I took in her pale pink lips, olive skin, sharp jaw, and the cute little button nose that softened her features. She was lean but curvy, with a generous rack that was barely contained by the modest bathing suit she wore underneath one of those flowered sarongs. I glanced down and inhaled as I realized that even her feet were cute, with bright blue polish on her toes. I automatically looked at her left hand, breathing a sigh of relief when I saw that her ring finger was bare.

My eyes raised up to meet her appraising gaze and in that moment I knew. This was the woman for me. I did not care who I had to kill, she would be mine. Judging from the shell-shocked look in her beautiful eyes, I wasn't the only one who felt like I had just been hit with a two by four.

Someone cleared their throat, breaking the little staring contest my dark-haired beauty and I were engaged in. I felt a flush rise up my face as I took in the amused gazes of the other women at the table.

"We'll have a pitcher of margaritas and four glasses," a woman with purple streaks in her hair told me. "And some chips and salsa please."

"Just water for me." My new love spoke for the first time, her voice cultured and firm. "I have to work."

"Teresa Ann Fontenot, you are not going to work here," Purple Hair chided. "You promised me you'd relax and have fun this weekend."

My girl shot an annoyed look at Purple Hair. "Fine, I'll have a drink, but just one."

"I can make you a virgin one if you'd like," I offered.

The other women at the table laughed like I'd said something funny. "Virgin? It's way too late for that," Purple Hair said teasingly. "What's your name, barkeep?"

"Colin."

"Hi Colin. I'm Evie. These are my friends Dawn and Emma," she pointed to each one in turn, then put her arm across the shoulders of my girl. "And this is my little sister, Teresa."

"Nice to meet you all, are you gals here to celebrate something?"

"It's Evie's fiftieth birthday," Emma responded. "We're here for a girls' weekend."

"Well, happy birthday. And thank you for choosing the Hamilton Keys Resort for your celebration trip."

I headed back to the bar to mix up their margaritas and send their food order to the kitchen. I could feel the ladies watching me as I worked. When I returned a few minutes later with their drinks, the birthday girl pounced.

"So, Colin," she drawled. "My sister hasn't had a vacation in many years. She was hoping someone could show her around the resort."

"No I wasn't," she protested. Teresa shot me a wry smile. "Ignore these old ladies."

"I would be happy to show you around. I get off in an hour."

Evie giggled and whispered something to her sister that I could swear was, "Say yes so you can get off too." It was nice to know the sister was on the same page as me.

I pointed at Teresa. "Don't disappear."

Then I moved back to the bar while I was still ahead, although my eyes kept going to Teresa every few minutes. She was watching me too, even though she tried to pretend otherwise. The women were halfway through their second pitcher of drinks when Javier, the nighttime bartender, arrived.

"How's it going, Boss?" he asked me. "Any problems?"

I knew he thought it was weird that as the owner of the resort I insisted on scheduling myself for shifts at the bar. God knows I had enough money to never work another day in my life. But I wasn't the type of guy who sat around in his big office bossing people around. The best way for me to understand the customer experience was to be out among them, so I tried to do a few customer service shifts throughout the resort each month. Incognito, of course. Every once in a while someone recognized me from the local tabloids or one of those "World's Sexiest Billionaires" articles, but for the most part, it was easy for me to just blend in if I was dressed casually.

"Awesome." I nodded to the table where my girl sat. "Keep an eye on that group. They're drinking fast."

Except for Teresa, that is. She was still sipping at her first glass, seeming to prefer water to the strong margaritas her sister and their other friends were drinking like it was their last day on Earth. They'd all be feeling that later. I knew they were only a few years younger than me, and at our age, we couldn't drink all day and party all night anymore.

I headed towards the group, laser focused on Teresa. I gave her my most charming smile. "You ready for that tour now?"

I grabbed her hand to help her out of the chair, and I felt a current of awareness run up my arm like I'd grabbed a live wire. Teresa gasped, her eyes going to where my hand touched hers as if she was trying to figure out what was going on.

"Go on Teri Bear," her sister slurred. "We'll see you at dinner. Or not."

The group cackled in the way that only drunk women could do. Teresa rolled her eyes, then turned to me.

"I only have an hour."

"Then we'd better walk fast," I replied.

# Teresa

I followed Colin out of the restaurant, silently cursing my sister. I should have expected her to pull something like this after our conversation earlier today. I'd flown down from New York while Evie and her friends came in from Virginia, all of us meeting at the airport to take a shuttle over to the resort.

It was a beautiful place on the beach, light and airy, with several restaurants and bars, and every outdoor activity you could think of. I had a bad feeling I was going to spend the entire weekend saying 'no' to my sister and her wild schemes. I mean, she was older than me and she wanted to go ziplining? No thank you. Although based on what I had seen so far, there was a good chance my sister and her friends would be too drunk the whole trip to do much of anything.

After arriving this afternoon, we had all gotten settled into our cabana. It was large and beautiful, with tile floors, comfortable furniture, and a Spanish theme that was no doubt a nod to the early settlers of Florida. We had two bedrooms, one on either side of the spacious common area, each with two queen beds. Emma and Dawn took one bedroom, and Evie and I took the other. The cabana also had a bathroom that was larger than my entire apartment in New York City, and a private patio with lounge chairs and a jacuzzi. It really was a lovely set-up.

The minute the bedroom door had closed behind us Evie announced, "You need to get laid."

I looked up from unpacking my suitcase. "Huh?"

"Promise me that you'll try to get laid this weekend."

"I'll promise you no such thing," I retorted. "Besides, I have work to do."

"No, you don't. Besides, you can't work. We don't have Wi-Fi in the cabana."

I looked at her suspiciously. "What kind of a resort doesn't have Wi-Fi?"

I saw a flash of guilt before she hid it. "It's optional in the cabanas," she said. "I chose the 'no Wi-Fi' option so we could all disconnect."

Fine, I could just find a place to work somewhere else in the resort. I knew there had to be Wi-Fi in the common areas. Or maybe I could figure out how to make my phone into a hotspot? That thought had scarcely crossed my mind when Evie walked over and put her hands on my shoulders.

"Look little sister, I'm worried about you. You work all the time. You never take a day off and I haven't seen you since last Christmas. Every time I see you, you look more stressed out. Can't you try to just enjoy our weekend together without worrying about work? Please?"

I pulled her into a hug. "I'll try, Sis. I promise."

And now here I was, trailing a strange man as he showed me around and told me the history of the resort. I studied him covertly from the corner of my eye. He was incredibly hot. He was about four inches taller than me, with wide shoulders and a trim waist. He was wearing shorts, giving me a glimpse of his muscled calves. His hair was dark and thick, generously threaded with silver, and he was sporting a dark five o'clock shadow across his square jaw. It was his eyes that had caught my attention though. Dark and expressive, fringed by long lashes that women would pay good money for.

When our gazes met for the first time back at the bar, I had gotten the most uncanny sensation. It was like he somehow knew me, although we had never met. And when he touched me...I'd had to look around to see if I was standing on an extension cord or something. I'd never had such a strong physical reaction to a man before. It was unsettling.

Colin was an excellent tour guide. He walked me past the tennis court, the zipline entrance, the various buildings holding everything from reception to restaurants to the spa area, before leading me towards the beach.

"How long have you worked here?" I asked. He seemed very familiar with the resort and its history.

"Um. Since I was a kid."

At my curious look he added, "My dad worked here, so I followed him around a lot. He was a big believer in teaching kids the value of hard work at a young age."

"Then you worked your way up to bartender?" I asked. It seemed kind of weird that this guy had spent his entire career in one place. He had to be in his mid-forties, at least.

There was a flash of something in Colin's eyes that I could not interpret. "I actually...well, I'm a...I'm a floater. I work wherever I'm needed in the resort."

I had the feeling that wasn't what he was going to say originally, but who was I to ask a bunch of questions? The poor guy had been roped into giving me a tour after a long day of work. There'd been no way he could have said no without looking like a jerk to my sister.

"Over here is where you rent snorkeling equipment and sign up for parasailing," he said, pointing at a small building down the beach from where we were. "In this direction, you can walk for a couple of miles before you run out of beach. It's truly the best place to watch the sunset."

Suddenly I tripped on my own feet, pitching forward. In a flash, Colin had moved in front of me to prevent me from falling. The man was incredibly fast on his feet. Strong arms gripped my biceps, holding me steady. I put out one hand, bracing it on his chest. Good lord, I could feel how muscular it was, even through his thin Hawaiian shirt.

We both froze, staring at each other. My heart was racing, and I could feel the awareness shimmering between us, making the air even warmer than it was.

"Sorry about that," I whispered, staring up into his dark eyes.

"I'm not."

Before I could ask for clarification, Colin lowered his head towards mine. I knew he was going to kiss me and appreciated the fact he was moving slowly enough for me to step back. I should definitely step back. I was going to do that any time...

The minute his lips touched mine, everything inside me stilled. All the swirling in my mind, all the lists, all the things I needed to do, it all just evaporated. One hundred percent of my attention was focused on kissing this man.

When I didn't pull away, he licked along the seam of my lips, demanding entrance. His tongue swept in, and I moaned against him, sliding my arms around his waist. Colin pulled me closer, aligning our bodies, as we relaxed into the kiss. We fit together perfectly.

Colin slid his hand up, sliding his fingers into my hair, tilting my head to deepen the kiss even more. One strong thigh snuck in between my own, and I shamelessly rolled my core against his bare leg. I was sure the bathing suit I wore under my sarong was already soaked from the arousal flooding my pussy.

Good Lord, I had never been kissed like this. I'd never had this sensation of the entire world fading away. And I had certainly never felt like I could lay some stranger down on the sand and ride him like there was no tomorrow.

Oh crap. Sand. The beach. The sudden realization that I was humping a stranger's leg in a public place made me pull away, gasping for breath. Colin's eyes were dark, almost black, and his chest was heaving, just like mine was.

"I..." I paused, unsure what I should say. Oh yeah, my sister. "I should get back. I promised my sister I would join her and her friends for dinner."

Colin studied me for a moment. "Can we get together later?"

I shook my head. "I appreciate the offer, but I'm here for my sister, not to hook up with someone." I twirled around, desperate to put some space between us. "Thanks for the tour."

As I racewalked away, I could feel his eyes watching me. If I put just a little bit more sway to my hips than I normally did, well, that was just the side effect of walking on the uneven sand.

# Colin

I felt a pang in my chest as I watched Teresa walk away. I was certain that she had felt it too, the sense that when we kissed it wasn't just a kiss, it was the beginning of something. Something big.

I wasn't sure what that meant for either of us. She had a life in New York, while my life was here. I certainly could work in another part of our family's business, but the Hamilton Keys Resort was my baby. I would hate to have to leave it. Well, I didn't have to decide right now. First, I needed to figure out a way to spend more time with Teresa.

The solution presented itself the next morning. I was walking through the open air dining room and spotted Teresa and her companions at a table, taking advantage of the breakfast buffet.

The sister and her friends looked a little rough, but Teresa looked bright and sunny in loose navy shorts and a white tank top that hugged her curves.

"Good morning ladies," I said as I approached their table. "How is everyone today?"

Evie groaned. "Some of us might have had a little too much tequila yesterday."

Teresa sent her sister a teasing look. "I told you guys to slow down. You're not college kids on Spring Break you know."

"I was going to take my boat out today," I interrupted. "I was wondering if you ladies would like to join me?"

"You have a boat?" Teresa asked in surprise.

Oops, I forgot she thought I was just the bartender. It was refreshing, having someone get to know me as me, not as the heir to the Hamilton Resorts empire.

"Actually, it belongs to the resort," I prevaricated. It was technically true. The boat was part of the resort holdings. "But I, um, get to use it. What do you say?"

I sent Teresa a beseeching look even while I felt guilty about lying. I wasn't particularly good at it either. I just wanted a chance to get to know my girl without the weight of my family name getting between us.

Evie gave me an appraising look over the top of her sunglasses. I had the distinct feeling that she knew that I was trying to get closer to Teresa and was on my side.

"Teresa, why don't you go ahead? You said you wanted to go out on the water. The rest of us can lay on the beach and read this month's book club selection until we feel better."

My girl shot her sister a look. "I came to spend time with you," she protested. "That's what you said you wanted for your birthday."

"Yeah but that was before I realized I can't drink like I'm twenty anymore. You go on ahead. You hate laying on the beach doing nothing." Evie raised a finger in warning and continued, "And don't you even think about telling me you want to get on your damned laptop and work."

I could see the hesitation on Teresa's face, the desire to go with me at odds with her desire to stay with her sister.

"We'll just go out for a couple of hours, and then I'll bring you back to your sister." I gave Evie a reassuring smile, silently letting her know I would take good care of her little sister. "Hopefully by then you ladies will be feeling better."

I held my breath while Teresa looked around, then made her decision. "OK, thanks Colin, a boat ride does sound fun."

It took a great effort to resist pumping my fist in the air to celebrate. I placed my hand at the small of Teresa's back and guided her towards the dock. Her skin felt warm under my hand.

"So, what happened last night?" I asked. "Those three look a little rough this morning."

"My sister and her friends worked their way through I don't even know how many pitchers of margaritas. They got so drunk that they propositioned every man in the place, including our busboy who I'm pretty sure is a minor. I had a hell of a time getting them out of the bar and back to our cabana."

"Are you all staying together?"

"Yeah, we're in one of the two-bedroom cabanas. Dawn and Emma are in one bedroom, and my sister and I are in the other." She looked up at me. "Do they give you staff lodging here? Or do you live in town?"

"Um, yeah, some of us live on site."

"That's nice. I've heard of management getting housing at resorts like this, but not the service staff."

Crap, I had been imagining bringing Teresa back to my condo, but if we did she was going to have a lot of questions. There was no way she would think my penthouse condo was staff housing. I really should tell her the truth about who I was.

Instinctively I felt like Teresa wouldn't really care about my money. It was clear from her clothing and what she told me about her career that she made good money. Not billions, of course, but enough for her to own a place in Manhattan. I had not seen her show any interest in hearing about which guests had money, nor did she drop hints that she was interested in someone taking care of her. Just the fact that she thought I was just a bartender and still wanted to spend time with me was an indication that she wasn't shallow. I wanted a future with her, so I had to come clean with her. Maybe after our boat ride.

"This is quite a boat," she said, looking around as we boarded. I kept the boat in good condition, and while it wasn't the fanciest you could buy, it was definitely high end. Honestly, it was my favorite possession.

I turned on the motor while Teresa settled onto the deck. Her hair flew around her head as we started to move. Half an hour later I pulled the boat into a little cove where we could float without being pulled out to sea and shut down the engine. The water was still, and the boat rocked gently. The only sound was the birds.

"Do you want to go in the water?" I asked. "I'm pretty sure they keep extra swimsuits downstairs in the cabin."

Teresa shook her head. "No thanks, I'm not much of a swimmer. But please, feel free to go in if you want to. I'll watch safely from here."

I shook my head. "We can just hang out here on the deck for a while and enjoy the sun. I can go into the water anytime."

I brought Teresa a bottle of water from the cooler and plopped down on the deck next to her. We'd laid out beach towels and slathered on sunscreen. It was a beautiful day. Not too hot, not too cold. We chatted for a while, then fell into a comfortable silence.

Sitting next to Teresa, I could feel the energy vibrating between us the longer the silence lasted. I turned my head to study her as she stared out at the water. I wondered if she felt the hum of awareness between us as strongly as I did. Feeling my gaze, she turned her head. Our lips were only a few inches away from each other.

I cleared my throat. "I want to kiss you again."

Her eyes widened slightly, and she licked her lips. "I guess I wouldn't mind that."

I smiled. "That's a rousing endorsement of my kissing skills. Was I lacking yesterday?"

"You were OK," she teased with a mock frown. "But you might need a little more practice."

"Let's practice together."

Our mouths met in a mash of lips and teeth, immediately turning hot. I shifted so that I could lower Teresa onto her back, then moved on top of her, kissing her deeply. She tasted like sunshine, and everything inside me knew that she was the one I had been waiting for my entire life.

Her hands lifted, fingers sliding through my hair, and I shifted enough to slide one hand down between us to fondle her breast. Teresa moaned against my mouth as I circled around her nipple over the fabric of her shirt, teasing it to a hard point.

She pushed against my chest, and I reluctantly broke the kiss. Disappointment flooded through me as Teresa sat up, panting. I told myself we were probably moving too fast for her. I needed to slow things down.

"I have two questions for you," she said, her voice husky.

Her expression looked serious, and it made me nervous. "OK."

"One, is this spot private?"

I looked around in confusion. "I think so. I come here all the time and I have never seen another soul around."

"Great."

She paused and I prompted her, "What's your second question?"

"Do you have a condom?"

# Teresa

I wasn't shy around men, but I also wasn't normally super forward like this. I usually liked to date a guy for a couple of weeks before moving into intimacy, but with Colin, things were different. I knew I was only here for a couple of more days, but I didn't care. This was probably my one chance to have a hot, uninhibited, no strings attached vacation fling with a sexy guy. I was not going to let this opportunity go to waste.

I tried to tell myself that it was just because I was horny. It had been over a year since my last relationship, and a girl could only do so much with a vibrator and a detachable showerhead. But the truth was it was more than just breaking a dry spell. There was something about Colin, something I didn't want to examine too closely, that made me feel like I would regret it for the rest of my life if I didn't sleep with him. Even if it was just this once.

Colin's jaw dropped almost comically when I asked about the condom. He recovered quickly, leaping to his feet with a speed that belied his age. He grabbed my hand to pull me up.

"Let's go into the cabin."

I followed him downstairs into the boat, impressed with how fancy it was inside. Below deck was a large bedroom area. There was a queen-sized bed, with tables on each side, and a comfortable sitting area with a small couch and overstuffed chairs. The perimeter featured built in drawers and shelves, and there was a single door that I assumed led to the bathroom. The entire place was decked out in sleek wood and high quality touches.

Colin dug into the bedside table and produced a condom, tossing it on the bedspread. He reached behind him and pulled off his t-shirt, baring an impressive chest. It was covered in dark hair with strands of grey, tapering off to a happy trail that pointed the way to his visible erection. I licked my lips. I hoped to God he knew how to use that thing.

I pulled off my tank top, then reached behind myself to unclasp my bra. I could practically hear my breasts sigh in relief as they fell free. The first thing I did every night when I got home from work was take off my damn bra. It was both a blessing and a curse to have big boobs. Colin stared at them like he was hypnotized, letting me know where he fell on the blessing versus curse debate.

"How about you take off your pants?" I whispered.

Colin shot me a smirk. "You first."

I called his bluff, shoving my shorts and panties down my legs in one big push. His eyes slowly traveled up and down my body. I may have sucked in my stomach and pointed my breasts at him, so sue me. I worked hard to maintain my figure, but even the fittest person eventually succumbed to gravity.

Colin stalked towards me, eyes burning with desire. As soon as he was in reach, I grabbed him by the waistband and relieved him of his shorts, and then his briefs. His cock popped out and bounced against his flat stomach, glistening with pre-cum. I dropped to my knees.

"What are you doing?"

I raised one eyebrow. "Wow, you are really out of practice if you're asking that question."

I leaned forward and licked him from root to tip like a lollipop. Colin groaned. "You don't have to..."

"I want to."

I took his thick cock into my mouth and wrapped one hand around his base. I used my hand to follow the movements of my mouth, licking and sucking. I could hear Colin's breathing becoming labored, and I reveled in the sense of power I felt in that moment. I lifted my other hand to cup his balls, and he leapt back, pulling out of my mouth.

"What's the matter?"

"Bed. Now," he ordered.

I gave him a pout as I climbed to my feet. "I wasn't done."

To my surprise, Colin surged forward, grabbed me by the waist, and lifted me up. I squealed as he took a few steps across the room and tossed me on the bed. I landed with a soft bounce, and before I stopped moving he was on top of me, kissing me deeply.

I slid my legs out from underneath his and wrapped my legs around his waist. The movement tilted my pelvis, bringing his cock in contact with my slippery folds. We both groaned.

Colin looked down, his expression more serious than I had ever seen it. "Are you sure?"

I met his gaze head on. "Put on that condom and fuck me. Please."

He rolled off of me long enough to slide on protection, then returned to his position on top of me. Colin grabbed my hands, pulling them over my head and securing my wrists in one hand. I wiggled against his hold, my excitement increasing.

"I want to take this slow, but I don't know how much longer I can wait."

"Don't take it slow," I responded instantly. I wrapped my legs tight against him, pulling him closer, and without another word he slid inside me. I felt wonderfully full. Colin became completely still.

"Fuck. You're so tight," he grit out. His body was shaking with the effort of holding back.

"Move. For the love of God Colin, please move."

He slid slowly back, almost all the way out, then slammed back into me. When I whimpered in approval, he repeated the action several times, using a long slow rhythm that was gradually driving me insane.

I tugged against his hold and when he released my hands, I dug my fingernails into his shoulders. "Faster," I ordered.

That seemed to break the last of Colin's hesitation. He began pounding into me roughly and I hugged him close, digging my nails into his back and holding on as best I could. I loved this feeling. I could feel the tingles starting in my core and as if he could already read my unspoken plea, Colin lowered his hand between us and pressed his thumb against my clit. A few firm strokes of his thick thumb against my swollen bundle of nerves was all it took to finish me off.

"Colin!"

My breath stuttered as an orgasm rolled through me, harder and stronger than I had ever experienced. I felt my body shake and spasm around him, but Colin was right behind me. He grumbled a line of obscenities before freezing on top of me for a second. In the next breath he pushed deeper, and his hips jerked as he came with a slow groan of my name.

We both stilled for a long moment, waiting for our heartrates to slow down. He rolled off me and reached for a Kleenex box on the nightstand. After wrapping up the condom, he tossed it on the table and rolled onto his back, pulling me into his side. I cuddled against him, resting my head against his shoulder as I came back into my body.

After a few moments of silence, I rubbed his chest with my palm. "Wow."

"Yeah," he responded. "Wow."

We must have both fallen asleep because when I heard my cell phone beep in my shorts, somewhere across the room, I startled awake.

"What time is it?" I asked groggily.

Colin glanced at his watch. It was an expensive brand that I recognized, and I had the fleeting thought that it was unusual for a bartender to be able to afford something like that, but I lost the thought as I heard Colin's response. "Five o'clock."

I sat up with a start. "Holy shit, I've got to get back. I promised to meet my sister for dinner."

He pulled me down for a fast kiss. "Let's go."

We quickly pulled on our clothes and headed back upstairs to the deck. I sat on one of the benches as Colin started the engine and directed us away from the hidden cove. I could feel his eyes on me, but I continued looking straight ahead, staring at the water as I replayed what had just happened.

What had I done? It wasn't like me to be so impetuous.

My time with Colin had stirred feelings in me, feelings I didn't want to examine too closely. They felt a lot like...love. I'd known the man for two days, so of course it was impossible. *You don't even know this guy,* I reminded myself. Even though it felt so real, I knew that I had to be falling into that classic scenario of confusing love and sex.

*Stop being an idiot,* I chastised myself. But later that night as I hung out with my sister and her friends, I felt surprisingly unsettled. What happened to the woman who had always had her head on straight, the one who never let her emotions get in the way?

*She fell in love,* a little voice whispered in my head. As much as I tried to deny it, I knew it was true. And that was a huge problem, because I was going home in two days.

# Colin

I sat in the office above the disco, staring down at the dance floor. My eyes found Teresa immediately, dancing in a group with her sister and their friends. Once again the three older women appeared to be drunk, while I could tell from here that Teresa was sober as a judge.

My mind wandered back to this afternoon. It wasn't like me to lose track of time. Or nap. Or have sex with women I had just met. Yet all of those things had happened today. If I'd had any doubts that she was the woman for me, they had all disappeared this afternoon. I wasn't a young man, and while I had never been a manwhore like so many of my friends, I'd had my fair share of lovers. But none of those experiences had affected me as deeply as my time with Teresa.

I needed to figure out a way to keep her here. I also needed to come clean about who I was. A lie of omission was still a lie, and while I appreciated the fact that Teresa liked me as a simple bartender, after everything that had happened on the boat today, it didn't feel right to continue to mislead her. If I wanted something long-term, which I did, I needed to share my full story.

But how to tell her? It wasn't like I could go up to her and say, "Hey Teresa, funny thing about me working at the bar. I also own it..."

Teresa herded the other women out of the bar, and I headed downstairs. I would just follow them to make sure she got them back to their cabana okay. I had to admit I was surprised that the other ladies were drinking again after their massive hangovers this morning. It wasn't like they were young anymore; Evie was turning fifty for cripe's sake. But somehow they'd all had an amazing recovery, feeling well enough to dance the night away.

I trailed behind them, keeping out of sight, until the ladies were all safely in their cabana. I settled on a bench nearby to think, or maybe it was just a premonition because not ten minutes later I saw Teresa come back outside and head right towards me.

"Hey Teresa."

She jumped, putting her hand over her heart. "Jesus Christ, you almost gave me a heart attack. What are you doing hiding there in the dark?"

I stood up to meet her, moving into the soft light that illuminated the walkway. "I saw you ladies leaving the disco. I just wanted to make sure you got home okay. What are you doing out here, anyway?"

She rolled her eyes and made an awkward noise. "I wanted to see if you wanted to hang out some more, but then I realized that I didn't have your phone number or anything, so I thought I would walk around and see if I found you. I mean, if you wanted to hang out again. No pressure. No pressure at all. I'm not trying to be clingy."

She was cute when she babbled nervously. My heart swelled with relief that she was missing me as much as I was missing her.

"Give me your phone," I instructed. "I'm going to text myself right now so we are connected."

"We don't have to..."

"Your phone," I ordered.

She unlocked it and slid it into my palm. I quickly texted myself from her number, feeling the vibration in my pocket as the text connected. "There, now you can call me anytime."

She laughed. "Well, I'm only here for one more day, so I don't know how much I'll be texting you." Teresa moved closer, putting her arms around my neck. "So, um, do you want to go back to your place and pick up where we left off?"

"Yes." I answered immediately, then realized my dilemma. I could not bring Teresa back to my penthouse without coming clean about who I really was. I selfishly wanted one more night with her knowing that she was seeing Colin the man, not Colin the billionaire resort chain owner. "I mean no."

She frowned. "Oh, sure, sorry, I didn't mean to presume..."

I pulled her closer, inhaling the soft scent of her jasmine shampoo. "No, that's not it. I want to but I, um, have a roommate. And you're sharing a room with your sister. That presents a problem. Maybe there's a room open in the hotel..."

"Can we go back to the boat?" she asked. "Or will you get in trouble with your boss?"

I gave her a smile. "You're a genius. Yes, let's go to the boat. Why didn't I think of that?"

I grabbed her hand, and we headed back towards the dock. Climbing onboard the boat, I led her back down to the cabin.

"Will you spend the night with me?" I asked. "It's very restful sleeping on the water."

Our eyes met and held while she made a decision. "Sure. Besides, you can't possibly snore louder than my drunken sister."

I laughed. "You'll have to tell me in the morning. How about some champagne?"

"You have champagne?" she asked in surprise.

"There's some in the fridge," I told her, pointing to the mini fridge in the corner. It was about half the size of a regular refrigerator, and I kept it stocked with drinks and snacks. "We also have cheese and crackers."

"Won't you get in trouble if you raid your boss's fridge?" she asked in concern. "I don't want you to lose your job."

"Don't worry about it," I assured her with another pinch of guilt. I needed to tell her the truth, but I didn't want to ruin the mood. "I can just replace what we use. Nobody will be any wiser."

She looked skeptical. "That champagne in your hand is like seventy bucks a bottle."

I gave her a smile. "Totally worth it."

"In that case, drink up. I have a feeling we are going to work up a sweat."

I woke up the next morning with Teresa sound asleep in my arms. We'd made love twice last night, once fast and once slow and leisurely, both times perfect. I was considering waking her up by eating her pussy, but then I glanced at my watch and sighed. There was no time for fun, I needed to get to work. I had a ten o'clock meeting with my board of directors.

Leaning down, I pressed a soft kiss on her cheek. "Teresa, sweetie, it's time to get up."

She groaned, rolling over to press her face into the pillow. "What time is it?" she mumbled.

"Nine fifteen. I'm sorry to wake you, but I have to go to work now."

She sat up, looking slightly panicked, and I remembered her waking up from her nap yesterday the same way. Did she always greet the day in panic? Or was it only when she slept longer than she thought she should?

"Nine fifteen? Holy crap, I never sleep this late."

I leaned forward and gave her a gentle kiss, resisting the urge to deepen it. "I guess I wore you out last night."

She gave me a sultry smile. "Yeah, you did. But I suppose I should go see how hungover those girls are this morning. I left Evie a note that I was going to see if I could meet up with you, but she will probably be worried if I don't turn up soon."

"You're a good sister."

"Not really." Teresa's expression turned troubled as she got out of bed and started pulling on her clothes. "Evie begged me to come on this trip together because my schedule is crazy, and she said she missed hanging out with me. The last few years, I'm lucky if I see her once a year. Then we get here and I'm spending most of my time with you instead."

Her eyes met mine. "Not that I haven't enjoyed it, don't get me wrong, I'm just afraid that I'm neglecting my sister."

Given the way her sister had pushed us together, I doubted that she would be that upset, but then again Teresa knew her sister way better than I did.

"Well, let's get you back to her then."

We walked back to the cabana hand in hand, and after kissing her soundly, I left her on the doorstep and headed back towards the hotel. It was time to shower and get to work.

# Teresa

"Well, well, well, the prodigal sister returns."

My sister and her two friends were sitting around the table, a ton of breakfast food spread out in front of them. It looked and smelled delicious.

"Good morning, did you guys order room service or something?"

Evie nodded. "Yeah, and we got extra for you little sister."

"We figured you worked up an appetite last night," Dawn snickered.

I grabbed a plate, filling it up with eggs, fruit, and a couple of slices of bacon, and poured myself a cup of coffee before answering.

"As a matter of fact, I did." I looked around with a smug smile. "Twice."

My sister was studying me carefully. "You like him, don't you?"

I sighed happily as I took a bite of bacon. It was perfectly crispy. I had to hand it to the resort, their food was excellent.

"I wouldn't have slept with him if I didn't like him a little."

Evie shook her head, still staring at me. "No, I mean you like him, like him."

"What are we, in middle school?" I asked. I looked around, disconcerted that now all three of them were staring at me.

"Quit deflecting, Teri Bear."

"The truth is, yes, I do like him. I like him a lot. But it doesn't matter. He's a bartender in Florida and I'm a marketing executive in New York City. Even if we didn't live fifteen hundred miles away from each other, we have only known each other for three days. It's ridiculous to think about this being anything more than it is: a simple vacation fling."

I took another bite of bacon, then rushed to interrupt before my sister could argue with me. 'What's on our agenda today, birthday girl? I'm all yours today."

I spent most of the day on the beach with Evie, Dawn, and Emma. They'd gone ziplining yesterday while I was out with Colin, but after another night of drinking and dancing, they decided that they just wanted to take it easy today.

We pulled our loungers under a big, thatched umbrella that provided some shade, and just relaxed with our books. Every once in a while one of us would make a run over to the outdoor bar to get us drinks or a snack, but otherwise our little group just read quietly, napped, or stared out at the ocean.

I spent my time reading a book my sister had loaned me and trying not to think about my night with Colin. Evie owned a bookstore and every month she offered a "Boozy Book Club" where a bunch of women got together in the upstairs café to discuss a book and try different kinds of drinks that they paired with the stories. It sounded fun, and I almost wished I lived closer so I could join them for the book club. I worked so much I hardly got a chance to read, even though I loved it.

This month the Boozy Book Club members were reading a cozy mystery and even though I wasn't normally a fan of the genre, I was really enjoying the book. The premise was that a mystery man comes to a small town right when a murder occurs. The local octogenarians who hung out together at the senior center were on the case, revealing his true identity and solving the murder mystery in between their crazy hijinks. Even though I tried to figure out who the killer was, the author surprised me, and I finished up the book with a smile.

When dinner time rolled around we got ready to celebrate my sister's birthday in style. We had made reservations at an upscale steak and seafood restaurant on site. The resort offered several different places to eat, most of them casual, and we saved the fancy one for tonight. It was more expensive, but since it was Evie's actual birthday today and our last night together before we all headed home tomorrow, we wanted to splurge and do something fancy.

We pulled on cute dresses and strappy sandals and took some time to fix our hair and make-up for our final night together.

"We all clean up pretty well for old ladies," Dawn said as we met in the living room.

I had to admit that she was right. I might be younger than the rest of them, but I was still firmly in midlife. Despite that, we all looked hot enough to turn some heads as we entered the restaurant. Of course, most of those heads were sixty year old men, but as they say, beggars can't be choosers.

We had a delicious dinner of surf and turf and drank our way through two bottles of wine then sang "Happy Birthday" to Evie. The entire restaurant joined in, and the waiter even brought her a little cake with a candle. By the time we were done we were all stuffed, and we decided to have an early night in the cabana. I was relieved that my sister didn't want to spend another night dancing in the disco. It really was not my scene.

As we walked out of the restaurant, we ran into Colin and another man in the lobby. They were both carrying briefcases and wearing expensive suits. I caught my breath at how handsome Colin was, dressed up with his hair slicked back into a more conservative style than he usually wore. I saw him check out my outfit, his eyes darkening in appreciation.

"Oh. Teresa. Ladies. I, um, I didn't know you were having dinner here tonight."

I cocked my head, wondering why he seemed so nervous. My eyes moved between Colin and the other man.

"Are you working in the restaurant tonight Colin?" I asked. "It didn't look busy enough in there for them to need a second bartender." It was nine o'clock on a Sunday night and the restaurant was mostly empty.

The man with Colin laughed. "Bartender? Are you still doing that 'I need to work in the trenches alongside my staff' thing? You're the only boss I know who does that."

"Boss?" I asked. I noticed a flush rise up Colin's face, and he looked everywhere but at me. "I didn't realize you supervised the other bartenders."

Colin's companion laughed again, loudly. He seemed like one of those typical rich obnoxious jerks I ran into all the time in New York. "He doesn't just supervise the bartenders honey," he said condescendingly. "Don't you know who he is? Colin runs this whole place."

Ignoring his rude companion, I looked at Colin. He had an expression on his face I couldn't quite decipher, it seemed to be a mix of dread and embarrassment.

"Colin. What is he talking about?" I could feel my sister move closer, instinctively knowing I might need support.

"I, uh, I own this place."

"You own the restaurant?" I asked in surprise. "It seems like that would have come up in our conversations."

"No. I own the entire resort. Well, my family does."

"What?" My tone rose to a higher pitch than I had intended, and Colin winced. "The resort? You own the whole resort?"

He nodded.

"And the boat? That's yours too?"

"Yes," he said sheepishly.

"You lied to me. I thought you were just a bartender."

"Well, I do take a couple of shifts a month in the bar. But most of the time, I'm running the business side of the resort."

"And all the other resorts in your portfolio," the other man added. He looked curiously between us. "Are you guys dating or something? Did you really have no idea who this guy is?"

"I still don't know who he is," I snapped.

"He's Colin Hamilton. He and his family own the entire Hamilton Resorts chain. Over twenty resorts around the world."

My heart was thumping as a sense of betrayal filled me. I recognized the Hamilton name. Of course, who wouldn't? They were one of the wealthiest families in the country. Why would Colin have lied to me? Why did he let me think he was just a bartender when he was really a billionaire? Was this some kind of game he played with tourists?

I felt my breath coming in quick pants and my sister thankfully came to my rescue. She shot Colin a glare and took my arm. "Come on, sis. Let's go back to our cabana."

When we got back to our place I went right to our room and collapsed face down on the bed. I couldn't decide how I felt. Part of me was angry and embarrassed at Colin for lying and making a fool of me. Part of me was hurt. And part of me was making the realization that I had fallen in love for the first time in my life, and it wasn't real. At least not for him.

My sister crawled into bed with me and held me close, the way she used to do when we were kids.

"I'm so sorry Teri Bear, I didn't know he would turn out to be a rat when I pushed the two of you together. I just wanted you to have some fun, maybe fall in love."

"Love isn't in the cards for me, Evie," I said sadly. My eyes were burning with the effort of holding back tears.

She patted my shoulder. "You don't need a man to have a good life, but it is nice to have companionship." Her tone turned wistful. "I wouldn't mind someone to warm my bed and make me breakfast and kill spiders."

I rolled my eyes. "You're a successful businesswoman. You can make your own breakfast and kill your own spiders."

"Yeah, but I don't want to."

# Colin

After I finished up my dinner meeting with that jackass John, I spent a restless night tossing and turning. I hadn't expected Teresa and her friends to show up at that particular restaurant. They had stuck to the more casual dining options the rest of the trip, so I naively believed it would be a safe place to have my meeting. In retrospect, I should have just had the staff bring dinner to my office conference room.

John was a friend of my father's and a partner on several business ventures. He was also a pompous asshole. He'd thought it was hilarious that Teresa believed I was a bartender, so hilarious that he ribbed me about it for a good ten minutes before I told him to shut up.

"Why are you so sensitive?" he'd asked me. "I totally get why you would want to play poor bartender. I was a bartender in college, and it was a great way for me to get laid by slutty co-eds. She's a little older than a co-ed, but she's quite a looker."

"Don't talk about Teresa like that," I'd bit out. "She just assumed I was the bartender, and I let her go on believing it because it was nice to know, for once, that a woman liked me for myself and not for my name or my money."

John stared at me for a long moment, his gaze appraising. "You really like her, don't you?"

"Of course I like her."

"I mean as more than a fling or some easy lay. I thought she was just some tourist you were having fun with."

I bit back the urge to punch him for even implying something like that about my Teresa. "My feelings for her are none of your business."

He nodded. "Yeah, that answers my question. Well my friend, I wish you good luck with your lady love. I hope you can work it out with her. Take it from me, you don't want to spend your later years all alone."

When we finished our business it was after eleven, so I decided to wait to see Teresa in the morning. I wanted to apologize. I wanted to explain why I let her think I was just some random bartender. I wanted to beg her to consider staying, or to commit to a long-distance relationship until we figured out a plan to be together. I wanted to tell her that I loved her.

Unfortunately, I was too late.

Evie greeted me at the door with a stern glare when I knocked just after nine o'clock. I could see their suitcases lined up near the door. I remembered Teresa telling me that they were leaving today.

"Oh, I thought you were the shuttle driver." She put her hands on her hips and looked at me like I was something she'd just stepped on. "Oh wait, are you pretending to be a shuttle driver today?"

"Can I speak with Teresa please?"

"You're too late Mr. Liar McPants on Fire."

"I didn't lie, exactly." I don't know why I was defending myself. I was totally a liar. "I mean, I know it was a lie of omission. But I can explain." I looked past Evie at her two friends but didn't see Teresa.

"Teresa!" I bellowed. "Please, can we talk?"

"I told you, you're too late. She left this morning."

"What?" I searched Evie's face, trying to determine if she was telling the truth.

"It's Monday, and my dear sister was in a hurry to get back to her desk in New York in time for work. She flew out on a five a.m. flight."

"Shit."

I dropped my head to my chest, fighting the urge to punch the wall. Or cry. Why hadn't I come over last night? It killed me that Teresa left thinking I was just playing her. I felt a touch on my arm and looked up to see Evie watching me carefully.

"Oh, you're really upset, aren't you?" She sounded relieved. "I thought this was more than just a fling, more than just some silly game you play with the tourists. I thought you had feelings for her – we all did—but after last night, well..."

I raised my eyes to meet her gaze, showing her that my words were true.

"I love her, Evie. She's everything to me."

Evie's eyes widened. "In that case, you'd better come in so we can talk."

# Teresa

I trudged up the street to my condo, my feet feeling like lead. I had just finished the longest week of my life, and I wanted nothing more than to eat the Thai food I'd ordered before leaving the office, drink a cold beer, and go to sleep for the entire weekend.

After a long, heartfelt conversation with my sister about my feelings for Colin, I had gotten up early on Monday morning and headed back to New York City. The others were staying at the resort until early afternoon, but when we had made the reservations I had been eager to get back home in time to work a full day on Monday.

I had been sadder than I expected to say goodbye to my sister. Despite all the time I had spent with Colin on the weekend, I had also enjoyed the time I had spent hanging out with Evie and her friends, talking and reconnecting. As irritated as I had been with my mother for bullying me into going on the trip, I was glad I had gone. Even if I had gotten my heart broken.

I shook my head. How had this happened? It wasn't like me to be impetuous. I did everything with a plan and a list. I wasn't a person who slept with near strangers or fell in love at first sight. That was romance book ridiculousness. At least I thought it was, until it happened to me.

God help me, I did love Colin. I'd never in my life felt anything like it. Every time I thought about him I felt a twinge in my chest. I couldn't eat. I couldn't sleep. I couldn't concentrate on work. I had only gotten through the last five days with copious amounts of coffee and sheer determination.

Colin had texted me a couple of times the day I left, but I blocked his number without reading them. I didn't want to hear his excuses. Evie, bless her heart, had texted me every day to check on me. She really was a good sister. I resolved to make some time to go down and visit her. I wanted to check out her bookstore and attend one of their Boozy Book Club meetings. They sounded hilarious. Evie had promised to keep me up to date with what the rest of them were reading so we could talk about the books.

My condo was on the top floor of a three-story walk-up. There were only two units per floor, and they were relatively large by New York City standards. I loved my place, and I felt a lot of pride that I had been able to buy it totally on my own. Who said I needed a man to make me happy?

Speaking of a man, there was one sitting in front of my door when I came up the stairs. My eyes widened as I realized it was Colin. I wondered how he had charmed his way through the security doors. My neighbors were usually pretty good about not letting people in, that's one of the things I liked about this building.

"Colin? What are you doing here?"

"Teresa. Hi." He jumped to his feet and thrust a bouquet of flowers in my direction. Daisies, my favorite.

I sniffed them before returning my attention to him. "How did you know where I live?"

"I have my sources."

I raised my eyebrow and asked again. "What are you doing here?"

"Can we talk? I would like to explain. Please?"

I noticed that he looked pretty rough. His clothes were wrinkled, his hair was sticking up, and he had dark shadows under his eyes as if he had not been sleeping. He looked a little thinner too. I felt his pain. It was the same way I looked when I had checked myself out in the mirror this morning.

"What's the point of talking? There's nothing to say. We had a fling and now it's over. No hard feelings, OK?"

"It wasn't just a fling," he said stubbornly.

The door across the hall opened and my neighbor stepped out, looking at us curiously. "Are you OK, Teresa?" Mr. Ruiz asked. "Should I call the police?"

I gave him a smile. "Oh no, I'm fine Mr. Ruiz, but thank you for checking on me. Colin is...a friend."

He nodded but shot Colin a stern look. I almost laughed. Mr. Ruiz was like eighty years old, and clearly he was willing to beat up Colin if I needed him to. "Just call me if you need me, honey, and I'll come right over."

"I will, thank you."

I walked past Colin to unlock the door. "You might as well come in," I said grudgingly. I wasn't sure what he wanted to talk about, but it wasn't the best idea to have the conversation in the hallway.

Colin followed me in, looking around curiously. I saw him taking in the tasteful but comfortable furniture, the artwork on the walls, and the riot of plants along the windows. "Nice place you have here."

"Thank you." I walked over to the refrigerator and pulled out two beers. Uncapping them, I handed one to Colin and gestured to the small kitchen table.

"You have about ten minutes before my food comes and then you're done. Use your time wisely."

Colin took a long drink from his bottle, then leaned forward to meet my eyes. "I've missed you."

My heart fluttered, but I ignored it. "We barely know each other. What's to miss? Besides, I'm sure there will be another tourist you can play with soon enough."

A flash of pain crossed his face. "I want to apologize for misleading you. I was not playing with you. I know that there's no excuse for what I did, but I would like to explain."

When I didn't respond, he continued, "My family is quite well known in certain circles. In Florida in particular, a lot of people know me, know my family. People take pictures of me for the local gossip rags, and wherever I go, women...and sometimes men... pursue me."

"Must be tough to be popular," I said with uncharacteristic sarcasm.

"I learned a long time ago that people cozy up to me for my money. They don't care about me as a person, they only care about my wealth and my influence." He took another sip of his beer. "It's a weird feeling, never knowing if people like you for yourself, or just what you can do for them. Over the years, I have learned to be cautious, to choose my relationships wisely."

Colin reached across the table and took my hand in his. I didn't have it in me to pull away. The hum of electricity that was always between us felt oddly comforting after my long week alone.

"When I realized that you and your friends had no idea who I was, well, it was so nice to be a regular guy, you know? I didn't intend to mislead you, but it was such a great feeling, just for once, to know that someone liked me for me. To know there was no ulterior motive, that it wasn't about my money or my family name. I kept telling myself that I needed to come clean with you, that it was ridiculous for a forty-eight year old man to be pretending to be someone else, but I didn't want to do anything to make you look at me differently."

"So, what was your plan?" I asked. "To let me leave thinking I'd had a fun vacation fling with a handsome bartender?"

"You think I'm handsome?"

I rolled my eyes, then looked pointedly at my watch. "You've got about five minutes before I kick you out, buddy."

"My plan was to finish my business meeting with that insufferable asshole John, then come to your cabana and ask you to take a walk on the beach with me so I could tell you who I really was. I didn't anticipate running into you, having you find out like that." He met my gaze, his eyes earnest. "I swear I was going to tell you before you left."

"Don't worry about it, it's fine. I'm fine."

"Are you?" He eyed me with concern. "You look tired."

I sighed deeply. "I've had a long week. Look Colin, I appreciate you coming all the way up here to tell me why you did what you did, but you didn't need to. The truth is, I understand why you did it, now that you've explained. I don't have any bad feelings towards you, honestly."

"But you do have feelings?"

"What?"

"I'm asking if you have feelings for me." He held up a hand before I could answer. "Because I have feelings for you, Teresa. I didn't just come here to explain and apologize. I came here to tell you that I love you."

My heart literally stopped in my chest. Colin loved me? Was he telling the truth? The sound of knocking on the door broke the silence in the room. Without a word I got up and opened the door, grabbing my food from the delivery guy. I dropped the bag of food on the table between us, my mind racing as I replayed his words.

"You love me?"

Colin nodded. "I do."

"We only spent three days together. That's impossible."

"I only needed three minutes with you to know that you are the woman for me."

My mouth dropped open. "We're not kids anymore Colin, and this is not some romance book that my sister reads in her book club. There's no such thing as instalove. Grown-ups don't fall in love in three days."

"Who says they don't?" he countered. "We're not kids, so we know our own minds. We know what we want. I have never felt this way before. I have no doubts at all. I love you and I want us to build a life together."

"We live fifteen hundred miles away from each other."

"I could move here."

I shook my head. "Your job is in Florida."

"I could commute on the weekends. Or you could move down to the resort. We have a marketing director position open."

"I'm not going to move fifteen hundred miles away after three days together, and I'm certainly not going to take some job because I'm the owner's girlfriend." I stood up and started pacing back and forth. "I just don't see how this could work."

Colin stood up and put his hands on my shoulders. "Do you love me Teresa? If so, we can work this out, I promise you. Just...please tell me that I'm not alone in this."

I looked into his eyes and couldn't bear to lie. "You're not alone," I whispered. His eyes lit up in relief.

"Then how about this? We agree to date long distance. You can check out the job at the resort – and other jobs in the area – and if you find something you're interested in, I give you my word I won't interfere. If you get a job in Florida I promise it will be completely on your own merit. And if Florida doesn't work out, I'll figure out a way to work remotely from New York."

"This is crazy."

Colin cupped my face in his hands. "Love is crazy Teresa, that doesn't mean it's not true."

For the first time in my life, I did something that I didn't plan. I didn't analyze all the options. It was scary as hell, but somehow it felt right. I decided to take a chance on love.

"If you ever lie to me again Colin, even by omission, I promise you that you will never get another chance with me."

He nodded. "Believe me, your sister and her friends already warned me that if I hurt you again they'd cut off my dick and choke me with it."

I burst out laughing. "Yeah, that sounds like my sister all right. So, what happens next?"

"How about you share your Thai food with me, and then we'll have make-up sex?"

"I don't know, I really love Thai food. I'm not sure if I want to share it."

"Not even with the man you love?"

I leaned forward until our lips were almost touching. "Maybe just this once."

# Epilogue – Colin

*Six months later...*

"Welcome home Mrs. Hamilton, how was work today?"

Teresa kicked off her heels by the door and padded over to give me a kiss. "It was great." She looked around with a smile. "You cooked?"

"Well, technically I ordered us food from the restaurant." I wouldn't lie to her. Not ever again.

Teresa laughed. "That's a good choice. I love you, but you're a terrible cook."

"Hey, I can grill. And I make a great breakfast."

"Yeah, that's true. Your scrambled eggs and bacon are passable." She gave me a wink to let me know she was kidding.

After two months of one of us flying to see the other every weekend, Teresa had decided to take the leap and move to Florida so we could move in together. She had been resistant about applying for a position here at the resort, but our Chief Operating Officer had finally convinced her that she wanted Teresa for her team because of her skills, not who her boyfriend was. We had all agreed that I would not get involved in my wife's job in any way. The truth was that Teresa was very well known in the marketing world and it was a huge coup for the Hamilton Keys Resort to get her on staff. She had gotten several offers from businesses who had tried to steal her away from us.

We'd had a surprisingly easy transition into living together. I had never been so in sync with someone before. We shared the household chores and enjoyed reading together and going out on the boat on our days off. We were both working fewer hours now too. We were committed to spending time together and having better work/life balance.

Even after several months together, our passion was as strong as ever. I swear we both had the stamina of a couple half our age.

The weekend after she moved in with me I proposed to her. Some people might have thought we were rushing things, but we knew what was right for us. We agreed to have a small informal wedding on the beach, just with our closest family and friends. Evie was her maid of honor, and my father stood up for me. My whole family loved Teresa and she had fit right in with us like she'd always been there.

The day we got married was the happiest day of my life, and I had spent every day since then thanking the universe that Teresa had wandered into my bar with her sister. She was perfect for me, and I was committed to making her as happy as she made me.

"Oh, you got a package. It's on the coffee table."

Teresa retrieved the package and ripped open the envelope. A book fell out and she smiled. Her sister had taken to sending Teresa the book that her book club was reading each month. It was a nice way for them to connect, talking about what they liked about each book.

"The Billionaire's Curvy Assistant." Teresa rolled her eyes. "I don't think I'm going to like this one very much. I'm not a big romance fan."

I looked at the handsome man on the cover. He was wearing a suit and adjusting his cufflinks. Honestly, he looked like a douche. I grabbed the book from her. "You've got your own billionaire, baby."

"I don't know, I think I liked you better as a bartender."

I pulled her close and kissed her until we were both breathless. "Are you sure about that?"

She laughed. "The truth is, I like both sides of you. The laid back bartender and the savvy businessman."

"Like?"

"Love, definitely love."

"I love you too, wife. Now, let's have dinner so I can give you something special for dessert."

"Cheesecake?"

I gave her a lascivious look. "I've got something else creamy in mind."

She punched my chest lightly. "Pervert. Let's eat."

***

Thank you for reading "Beach Reads". I hope you enjoyed Teresa and Colin's story. <u>Check out the rest of the Boozy Book Club series</u>[1] and follow along as Evie, Dawn, and Emma find their own true loves. Be sure to sign up for my mailing list[2] to be notified of all my new releases and special sales. I will even give you a free book!

---

1. https://bit.ly/AuthorRoseBak

2. https://storyoriginapp.com/giveaways/62ee758e-068f-11eb-904e-c373f6014fe1

# Special Preview

## Until You Came Along by Rose Bak

Jen heard the rumbling from all the way in the kitchen. Wiping her hands on a towel, she walked to the front porch to watch the two large buses drive up the long driveway to the farmhouse. Belching smoke, they idled and came to a stop, one behind the other.

Although it wasn't even 10 a.m. yet, the sun shone brightly in the summer sky, showcasing the dust left in the wake of the parked buses. A bird squawked loudly in the sudden silence as a serious looking young woman scurried out of the first bus, glasses askew, a clipboard gripped in one hand, cellphone in another. Two large mountains of men followed her, hulking shadows.

"Jen Oliver? The band is here. We'll just come in and...." she moved to enter the house, but Jen stood her ground, blocking the door.

"Where are they?" she asked the woman, her tone icy. "And who are you exactly?"

The woman looked flustered for a brief moment before her stern mask fell back down again. She shuffled her cell phone into the hand with the clipboard and stuck out her now-free hand to shake. "I'm Simone. I manage the band."

Jen ignored her hand. "Well, manage them out of those buses. They don't get to send the help out to greet their sister."

Simone looked confused as she dropped her hand back to her side. "They're all sleeping. They had a late night. We'll just come in and check...."

"Still up all night and sleeping all day, huh? That's been the same since they were teenagers." Jen shook her head. On the farm they had all been taught the value of hard work – up before dawn, work all day, and early to bed. Somehow those lessons hadn't really stuck with her brothers despite her grandparents' best efforts over the years.

Of course, the boys, as she still thought of them, had been away from the farm for ten years now, chasing fame and fortune as the biggest boy band to hit the charts since N Sync. Like the band that came before them, the Oliver Boys had grown up but continued to enchant teenage girls across the world with their pop tunes.

Simone clearly felt protective of the boys. "They played last night in Wichita you know," she said sternly. "The show went until almost midnight, then they met the fans and press for hours after."

"By meet the fans and press do you mean got drunk and partied?" Jen's tone did little to hide her opinion of the boys and their reputation for debauched partying.

Simone shook her head. "They've mostly settled down now. There's not as much partying as there used to be when they were younger. But they still need to make an effort to meet people, it's part of the job. Now we'll just come in and...."

Jen shook her head. "Well," she drawled. "When they wake up from their so-called job, you send them on in. The rest of you need to find some other place to bunk. I'm not running a hotel for drunken roadies here."

A slight movement behind Simone caught Jen's eyes. One of the giant men flanking Simone shook with repressed laughter, his mouth twisted in a smirk but his face otherwise impassive. Jen looked at him for the first time. He was the size of a small tank, several inches over six feet tall, with impossibly wide shoulders and large biceps. His hair was a dark blond, "dishwater blonde" her grandma would call it, worn military short. He was dressed all in black, and she noticed a gun on the shoulder holster. Jen wondered why he felt he needed a gun out here in the middle of nowhere. She felt him watching her and she raised her eyes to his, a shiver of awareness coursing through her, although she couldn't make out his eyes behind the dark sunglasses.

"Miss Oliver..." Simone started again.

"Jen"

"OK, then, Jen, we need to do a security sweep before the boys come in. If you could just move aside, we'll get started." Simone nodded decisively.

"A security—-what the hell are you talking about?"

Simone turned to the man who'd been staring at Jen earlier. "This is Nick, he's head of security for the band. He'll be doing a security sweep and assessment with Brian here," she pointed at the second silent man.

"We don't need a security sweep. This place is as safe as it comes. We don't even lock the doors in these parts."

Simone shook her head again, vibrating with irritation and clearly not used to people disobeying her orders. "No way. The boys don't go anywhere without a security check ahead of time. I'm afraid I have to insist."

Jen shot her a look filled with venom, her tone as cold as ice. "You can insist all you like but this is my property. You have no right to it, and neither do the boys. Y'all can just run along now, I'm not having some ginormous strangers poking around my property. Don't make me sic the dogs on you." Simone's mouth dropped open.

This was an empty threat. Jen's three dogs looked mean, but they were incurably friendly. They were just as likely to lick a person to death as bite them. Jen had a sneaking suspicion that if someone tried to kill her the dogs would jump over her body and leave with the killer. But these music people didn't need to know that. If there was one thing Jen hated, it was music people. They were way too self-important and proud.

"Excuse me ma'am," the guy called Nick interrupted.

"Jen," she repeated, a trace of irritation in her tone.

He inclined his head. "Sorry. Jen. As Simone mentioned, I'm head of security for the band. We've had some issues and I would be very appreciative if my team could just poke around for a bit and make sure there's nothing amiss." His tone was deferential and charming, which only heightened Jen's suspicions.

"What kind of issues?"

"I'm afraid I'm not at liberty to discuss that ma—I mean Jen."

"Then I'm afraid I'm not at liberty to grant you access to my property. You step foot off that driveway, and I'll shoot you myself, right after I set the dogs on you. And you," she pointed at Simone, "better make sure no one bothers me again until I see those boys on my porch." She spun on her heel and slammed the door. It was going to be a long day.

***

*For more of Jen's story, check out Until You Came Along by Rose Bak. Available at select online retailers here[1].*

---

1. *https://books2read.com/u/4A5kKe*

# Other Books by Rose Bak

**Boozy Book Club Series**
Beach Reads
Bubbly & Billionaires
Martinis & Mysteries
Bourbon & Bikers
**The Good with Numbers Holiday Romance Series**
Love Unmasked
The Thanksgiving Scrooge
Maid for Christmas
Countdown to Love
Valentine's Lottery
**Bite-Sized Shifters Paranormal Romance Series**
Long Distance Wolf
Wolf Doctor
Kat's Dog
Designer Wolf
Wolf Sheriff
Cocktail Wolf
Second Chance Wolf
**The Oliver Boys Band Contemporary Romance Series**
Until You Came Along
Rock Star Teacher
Rock Star Writer
Rock Star Neighbor
Rock Star Lawyer
**Loving the Holidays Contemporary Romance Series**
Dating Santa
New Year's Steve
Independence Dave
Comfort & Joy

**Holidays with the Shifters Series**
Santa's Claws
Bear Humbug
Jingle Bear
Silver Paws
Joy to the Wolf
Lion's Heart
**The Diamond Bay Contemporary Romance Series**
Brand New Penny
Fresh as a Daisy
Right as Rain
**Reunited Series**
Together Again
Finding My Baby
**Standalones**
Beach Wedding
Jessie's Girl
Summer Wedding
Faking It with the Detective
Christmas Punch
Roasting with Rob
**Non-fiction**
What to Do If You Find a Cougar in Your Living Room: Self-Care in an Uncaring World
It's All About Relationships: Reflections on Love, Friendship, and Connection

*Catch up with these and other stories coming soon. Join my newsletter for more information[1] or follow my author page on your favorite retailer.*

---

1. *https://storyoriginapp.com/giveaways/62ee758e-068f-11eb-904e-c373f6014fe1*

# About the Author

Rose Bak has been obsessed with books since she got her first library card at age five. She is a passionate reader with an e-reader bursting with thousands of beloved books.

Although Rose enjoys writing both fiction and nonfiction, romance novels have always been her favorite guilty pleasure, both as a reader and an author. Rose's contemporary romance books focus on strong female characters over thirty-five and the alpha males who love them. Expect a lot of steam, a little bit of snark, and a guaranteed happily ever after.

Rose lives in the Pacific Northwest with her family, and special needs dogs. In addition to writing, she also teaches accessible yoga and loves music. Sadly, she has absolutely no musical talent, so she mostly sings in the shower.

***

Please sign up for the Rose Bak Romance newsletter[1] to get a free book and keep up to date on all the latest news.

You can also follow Rose on Facebook[2], Instagram[3], Twitter[4], Goodreads[5], or Bookbub[6].

---

1. https://storyoriginapp.com/giveaways/62ee758e-068f-11eb-904e-c373f6014fe1

2. https://www.facebook.com/AuthorRoseBak

3. https://www.instagram.com/authorrosebak/

4. https://twitter.com/AuthorRoseBak

5. https://www.goodreads.com/authorrosebak

6. https://www.bookbub.com/authors/rose-bak

# Don't miss out!

Visit the website below and you can sign up to receive emails whenever Rose Bak publishes a new book. There's no charge and no obligation.

https://books2read.com/r/B-A-VATM-TOWAC

**BOOKS 2 READ**

Connecting independent readers to independent writers.

Did you love *Beach Reads*? Then you should read *Bubbly & Billionaires: A Midlife Instalove Romantic Comedy*[7] by Rose Bak!

**Falling in love with billionaires is only something that happens in romance books, right?**Nurse Emma Edwards is known for her bedside manner. Her quiet confidence and sunny personality can cheer up even the grumpiest patient.But her latest patient isn't just grumpy, he's successful, rich, and incredibly handsome. Wyatt Simmons made a fortune in business, but the widower is also quite lonely – at least until his daughter insists on hiring a nurse to care for him after emergency surgery. He might not want a nurse, but he does want Emma – for the rest of his life.They come from different worlds, but they're both old enough to know what they want – love."Bubbly & Billionaires" is book one in the "Boozy Book Club" series. Each story in the series is a steamy

---

7. https://books2read.com/u/baDyGx

8. https://books2read.com/u/baDyGx

standalone featuring a couple in their fifties, a nosy group of book club friends, matchmaking family members, and a sweet happily ever after that proves anyone can find love later in life.

Read more at https://rosebakenterprises.com/.